love flute

love flute

story and illustrations
by Paul Goble

Bradbury Press · New York

Maxwell Macmillan Canada   Toronto
Maxwell Macmillan International
New York   Oxford   Singapore   Sydney

Several steps were taken to make this an environmentally friendly book. The paper is made from not less than fifty-percent recycled fibers. The inks used are vegetable oil-based. Finally, the binders board is one-hundred-percent recycled material.

Library of Congress Cataloging-in-Publication Data   Goble, Paul.
Love flute / story and illustrations by Paul Goble. — 1st ed.
p.   cm.   Summary: A gift to a shy young man from the birds and animals helps him to express his love to a beautiful girl. ISBN 0-02-736261-2 1. Indians of North America—Great Plains—
Legends. [1. Indians of North America—Great Plains—Legends.]
I. Title.   E78.G73G65 1992   398.2′08997078—dc20
91-19716

REFERENCES: Hartley Burr Alexander, *The World's Rim*, University of Nebraska Press, Lincoln, 1953; Amos Bad Heart Bull and Helen H. Blish, *A Pictographic History of the Oglala Sioux*, University of Nebraska Press, Lincoln, 1967; Natalie Curtis, *The Indians' Book*, Harper and Brothers, New York, 1907; Ella C. Deloria and Jay Brandon, "The Origin of the Courting Flute," *W. H. Over Museum News*, Vol. 22, No. 6, Vermillion, 1961; Frances Densmore, "Teton Sioux Music," *Bureau of American Ethnology Bulletin* 61, Smithsonian Institution, Washington, DC, 1918; Richard Erdoes, *The Sound of Flutes*, Pantheon Books, New York, 1976; Alice C. Fletcher, *The Elk Mystery or Festival: Ogallala Sioux*, Peabody Museum of American Archaeology and Ethnology, Report No. 3, pp. 276–288, Cambridge, 1884; George Bird Grinnell, *The Cheyenne Indians*, Yale University Press, New Haven, 1923; William K. Powers, "The Art of Courtship among the Oglala," *American Indian Art* Vol. 5, No. 2, pp. 40–47, Scottsdale, 1980; Edward R. Wapp, *The Sioux Courting Flute*, M.A. Thesis, University of Washington, Seattle, 1984; William Wildschut, *Crow Indian Medicine Bundles*, Museum of the American Indian Heye Foundation, Vol. XVII, New York, 1975; Clark Wissler, "The Whirlwind and the Elk in the Mythology of the Dakota," *The Journal of American Folk-lore*, Vol. XVIII, No. LXXI, pp. 258–268, New York, 1905.

REFERENCES FOR THE LOVE FLUTE DRAWINGS: Sioux Indian Museum, Rapid City, pp. 11, 24 right, 30; The Shrine to Music Museum, Vermillion, SD, pp. 23 right, 24 left; State Historical Society of Iowa, Des Moines, pp. 9, 14, 17 left; Heritage Center, Miles City, MT, p. 6; Heritage Center, Red Cloud Indian School, Pine Ridge, SD, p. 23 left; Mille Lacs Indian Museum, Onamia, MN, p. 27; Buechel Memorial Lakota Museum, St. Francis, SD, p. 18; Crazy Horse Memorial, Crazy Horse, SD, p. 12; Plains Indian Museum, Buffalo Bill Historical Center, Cody, WY, p. 17 right; Denver Art Museum, Denver, CO, p. 29.

Remembering my father,
Robert Goble,
who helped to pioneer the
revival of making recorders
during the 1920s and 1930s.
This book is also for
my wife, Janet,
with all my love.

Tatuye topa makasitomniya le waku.

THANK YOU: Dennis Carter for your encouragement, and for sharing your knowledge of courting flutes.

THANK YOU: Emil Her Many Horses, curator of the Buechel Memorial Lakota Museum at St. Francis, South Dakota, for showing me the collection.

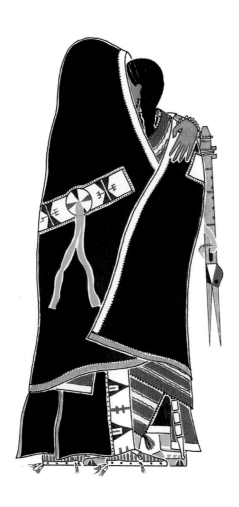

In traditional times the love flute, or courting flute, was only used by men to play love songs. It was not played for any other reason, and so it was mostly played by young men when courting, but some men serenaded their wives, and it has been recorded that a man's flute was wrapped with his body after death.

Courtship was formal, and carried on in front of everyone. There was little privacy in a tipi village; inside or outside the tipi, the only privacy was under a blanket, and what other people were polite not to hear or see. When a young man went courting he was scented and painted, and dressed in his finest, and in this he copied all the birds and animals. He carried a large blanket to wrap both himself and the girl he wooed. Partially tented under the blanket, standing there in plain view, whispering together, they felt alone. If the girl was popular, there might well be other suitors waiting in line! The blanket was made for him, with special wishes for his success, by his sister or a woman who was closely related. These and some of the other conventions of courting are mentioned in this book. The illustrations depict a time a little over one hundred years ago.

There are several different myths, or sacred stories, which tell how the love flute was given to people at different times and places; men have always needed supernatural help to attract, and to keep, the women they love! The ideas in this story are based on these, and on a Santee Dakota myth recorded by Ella Deloria and Jay Brandon, The Origin of the Courting Flute, *published in 1961 by the W. H. Over Museum at Vermillion, South Dakota. The flute was given by the Elk People. The bull elk is courteous and magnificent, and people saw how his cows loved him. A man wanted to be similarly chivalrous, and successful to attract the woman he loved. With his flute he felt and expressed the divine mystery and beauty of love, and the power of sexual desire. Although the flute had been given by the Elk People, it had also been imbued with the sounds and power of all living things, and so when a man played the flute, seeking to attract and to create new life, he did so as an integral part of all Creation.*

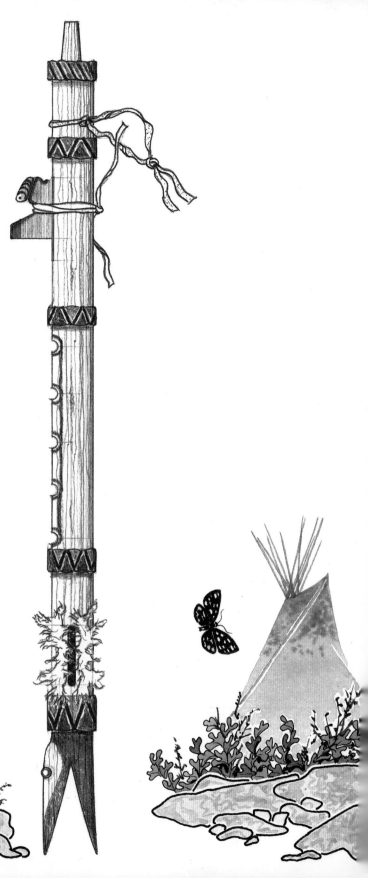

In the old days, melodies of flutes could be heard on summer evenings. They were love songs carried by the breezes into the tipi circle from the surrounding pine-covered ridges and grassy hills, where young men played on love flutes to the girls they loved. Each girl, at home under the watchful eyes of her parents, knew the tunes of the boy who loved her. Even though convention did not allow them to be together alone after dark, they were joined in spirit with the music of the flutes.

This is the story of a shy young man who was given the very first love flute, long ago, by the birds and animals.

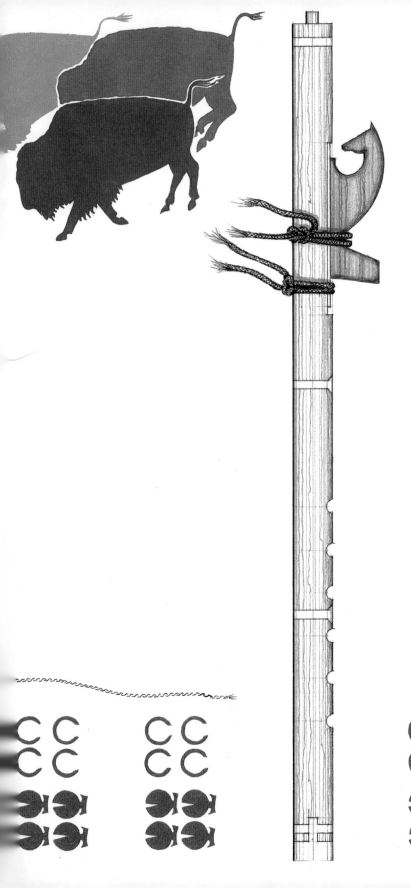

The young man was so shy that it was easier for him to face enemy warriors in battle than to speak to the girl he loved. Everyone knew he was brave.
He always led in the dangerous buffalo hunt, and yet he could never find the courage to tell the beautiful girl that he loved her. He was very unhappy with himself.

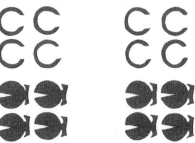

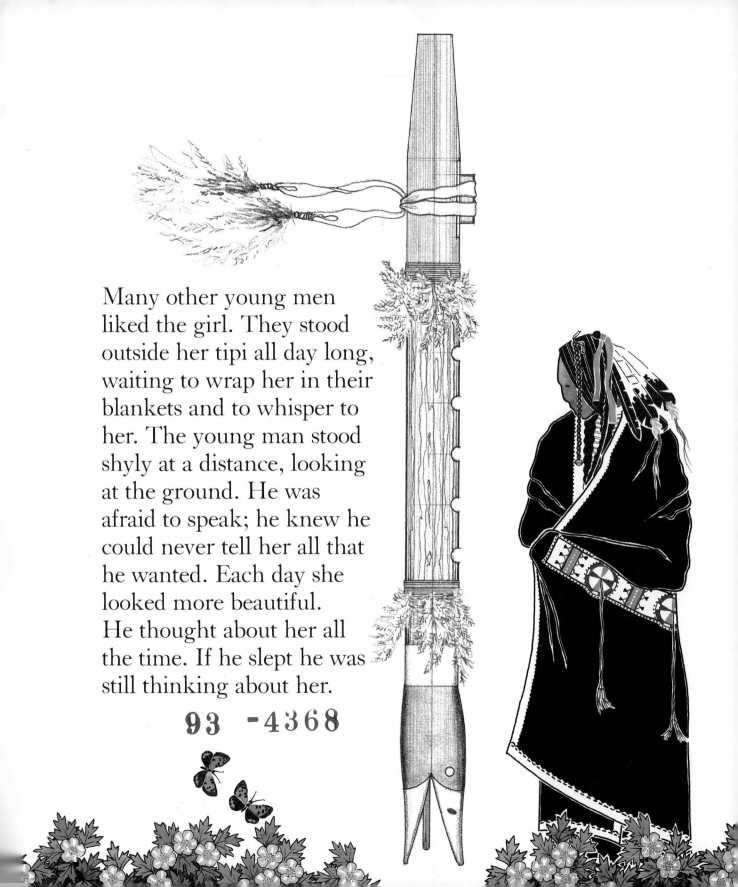

Many other young men liked the girl. They stood outside her tipi all day long, waiting to wrap her in their blankets and to whisper to her. The young man stood shyly at a distance, looking at the ground. He was afraid to speak; he knew he could never tell her all that he wanted. Each day she looked more beautiful. He thought about her all the time. If he slept he was still thinking about her.

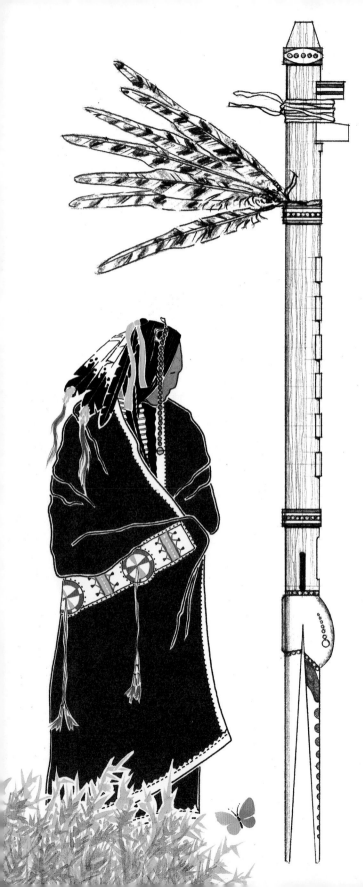

He waited by the river where she fetched water. There were always other young men waiting. He wished he was like them: they whistled to her, or threw pebbles into the water as she filled her water-carrier, and they hoped to wrap her in their blankets as she passed.

She smiled, and went on her way. They seemed to laugh and speak so easily with her.

"She smiles at us! She likes us!" they laughed among themselves.

The young man felt they spoke the truth. He thought she did not even notice him.

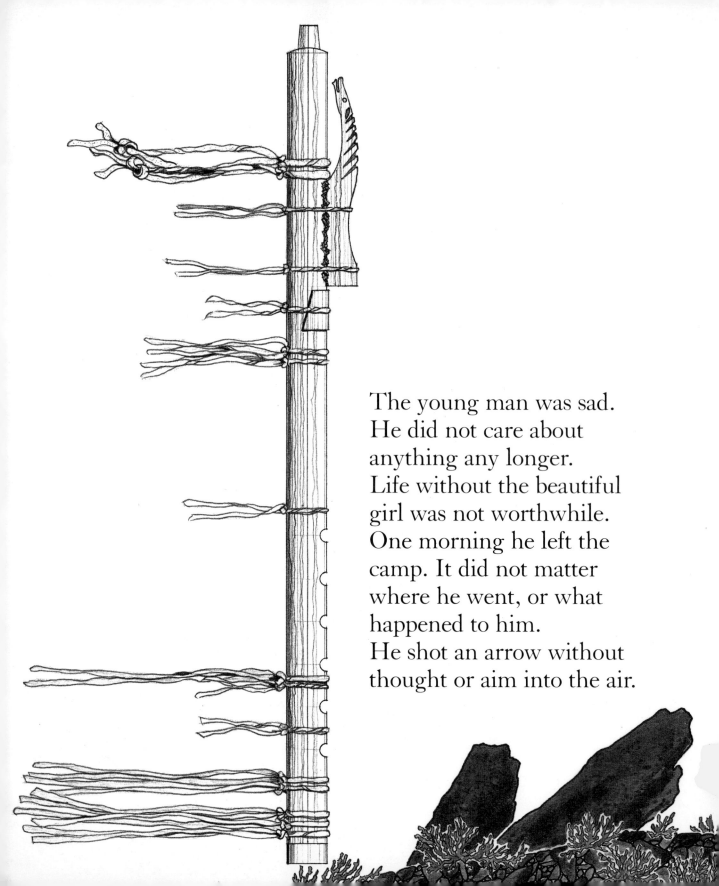

The young man was sad.
He did not care about
anything any longer.
Life without the beautiful
girl was not worthwhile.
One morning he left the
camp. It did not matter
where he went, or what
happened to him.
He shot an arrow without
thought or aim into the air.

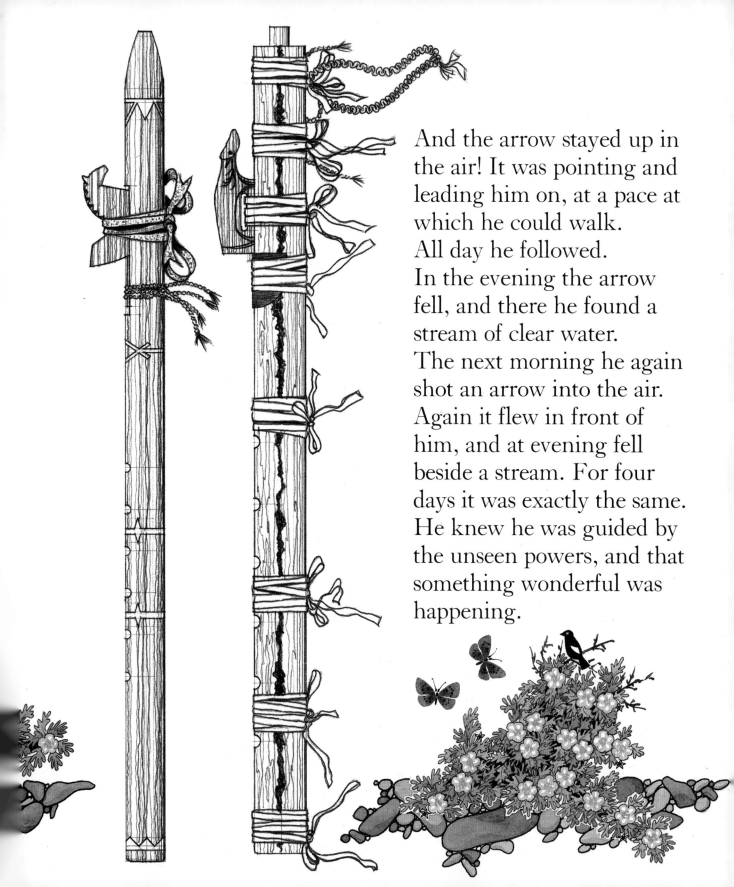

And the arrow stayed up in the air! It was pointing and leading him on, at a pace at which he could walk.
All day he followed.
In the evening the arrow fell, and there he found a stream of clear water.
The next morning he again shot an arrow into the air. Again it flew in front of him, and at evening fell beside a stream. For four days it was exactly the same. He knew he was guided by the unseen powers, and that something wonderful was happening.

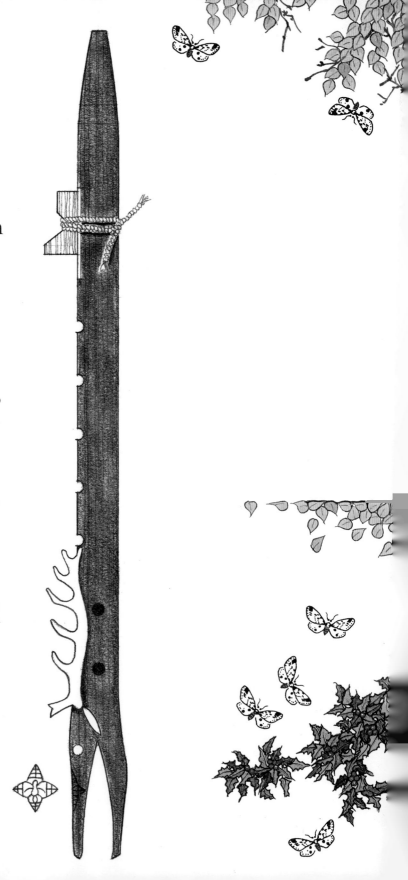

On the evening of the
fourth day he lay down to
sleep at the edge of an aspen
forest. The scent of yellow
leaves was good.
He was tired and sleepy.
Who can say whether he
was asleep, or still awake?
There was a rustle of leaves,
a click of hooves, and a
voice whispering: "Friend,
you tell him," and another
answering: "No, friend, *you*
tell him."
Two tall Elk Men with
branching antlers, and
painted black and yellow all
over, stood above him.

"We are going to help you," one of the Elk Men said. "We give you this: it is a flute. Listen!" He blew notes. . . .

Their sound was so beautiful that everything everywhere listened. All through the aspen forest the leaves trembled with gladness. The Elk Man said, "This flute is made of cedar wood, because cedars like to grow where the winds always blow. Woodpecker lives there; he made these five finger holes. See, he shaped his head at the end."

The other Elk Man said, "All the birds and animals have helped to make this flute for you. We have put our voices inside it. When you blow it, our harmony will be in your melodies. With the music of this flute you will speak straight to the heart of the girl you love. Your life together will be long, and you will have children."

The young man felt very
afraid of the Elk Men: their
eyes looked into him and
saw all his thoughts.
He had noticed that each of
them carried a hoop which
had a mirror at the center.
Suddenly they flashed the
mirrors into his eyes, and
he was blinded.
When he could see again
the Elk Men had gone.
Two bull elks were running
away into the trees.

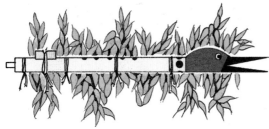

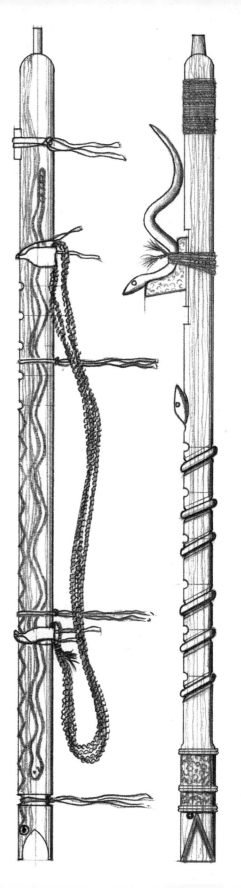

The next morning the young man found the flute, which the Elk Men had given him, lying on picked sage leaves.

Everything around him felt new and wonderful as he set off home again.

He blew on the flute, and the cranes joined in happy song.

He walked for four days, and all the while he listened closely to the songs of the birds and animals. Sometimes he blew into the flute, imitating their tunes and weaving them together until he had made his own melodies. Every bird and animal loved the songs he played.

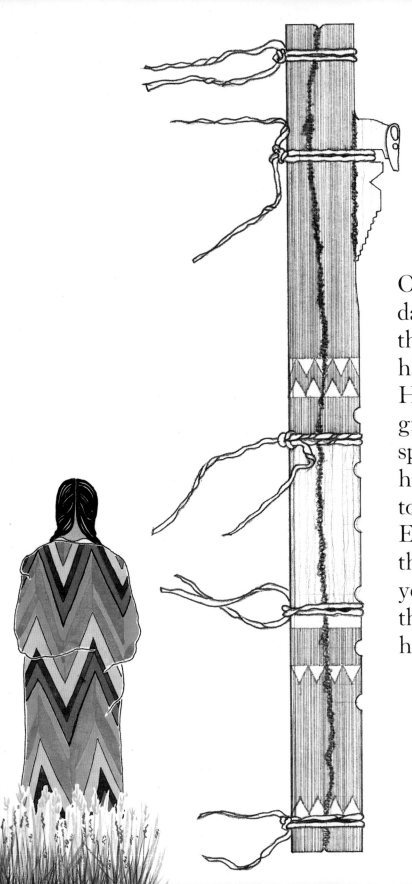

On the evening of the fourth day, when he came close to the camp, he began to play his flute.

He approached closer, and gradually closer, and the spirit of the breeze carried his wonderful songs straight to the girl he loved.

Every woman in the camp thrilled to the sound, and yet only the girl knew that the songs were speaking to her.

The girl left her tipi.
She loved the shy young
man who spoke to her with
the music of his flute.
He told her more
beautifully than words could
ever say:
I love you. I love you.
I love you. I love you.

Also by Paul Goble

Custer's Last Battle
The Fetterman Fight
Lone Bull's Horse Raid
The Friendly Wolf
The Girl Who Loved Wild Horses
The Gift of the Sacred Dog
Star Boy
Buffalo Woman
The Great Race
Death of the Iron Horse
Iktomi and the Boulder
Her Seven Brothers
Iktomi and the Berries
Beyond the Ridge
Iktomi and the Ducks
Dream Wolf
Iktomi and the Buffalo Skull
I Sing for the Animals
Crow Chief

SOUND RECORDINGS: For cassette tapes of traditional flute songs, similar to those which would have been heard in the old days, write to the Lakota flute player,
Kevin Locke
P.O. Box 241
Mobridge, South Dakota 57601.